BERTY'S STORY

Berty the Thirty is a shiny red tractor, a Massey Ferguson 35. He lives on a farm in Somerset and works hard for his owner Farmer Pete.

It is not a big farm, but there is plenty of work for Berty and his friend Fergus the Tractor, a Ferguson T20.

Berty has worked for Farmer Pete since he was a brand new tractor.

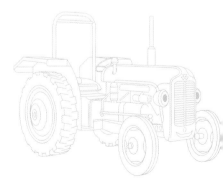

When Farmer Pete was a young boy his father, Farmer Bill owned the farm.

Farmer Pete spent all his spare time working hard for his father. He also helped other farmers nearby.

Farmer Pete was saving all his wages, so that one day he would have enough money to buy a tractor of his own.

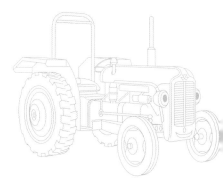

One day Farmer Bill said to his son, "Pete I am getting old and I cannot work as hard as I used to. It is time we changed places, you can run the farm now and I will help you."

Farmer Pete was pleased to have his own farm to look after at last.

He knew he must work very hard and to do this he would need a new tractor.

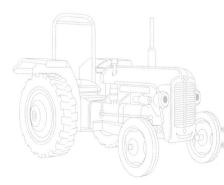

Farmer Pete visited some tractor showrooms, to see if he could find a tractor that he liked.

In one showroom he saw a shiny red Massey Ferguson 35.

He looked around the tractor and stroked its paintwork. He sat in the seat to see if it was comfortable and patted the tractor on the bonnet.

The shiny red tractor liked this. If Farmer Pete bought him he knew he would be looked after and be happy.

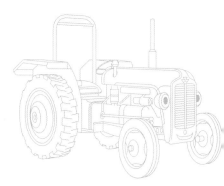

Farmer Pete went to the bank to see how much money he had saved.

The Bank Manager told him he had saved just enough money to buy a new tractor. He would not be able to buy the biggest, most powerful tractor, but he might just get the one he really wanted.

Farmer Pete took all of his money from the bank and went straight to the tractor showroom.

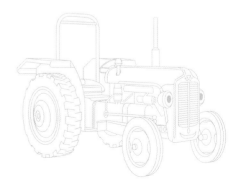

Farmer Pete was pleased to see the shiny red Massey Ferguson was still for sale.

The shiny red tractor was happy to see Farmer Pete again. He hoped so much that this farmer was going to buy him.

Of all the farmers that had looked at him he liked Farmer Pete the most.

The Massey Ferguson tractor closed his eyes
and held his breath.

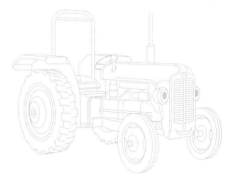

Farmer Pete patted the Massey Ferguson 35 on the bonnet.
He said to the salesman, "how much is this tractor?"

The salesman told Farmer Pete the price. Farmer Pete had already counted his money and knew that he had enough to buy him.

Farmer Pete said, "I accept, fill him up with fuel please, I will take him now."

The shiny red tractor opened his eyes and let out a big sigh of relief. He was so happy that Farmer Pete was going to buy him.

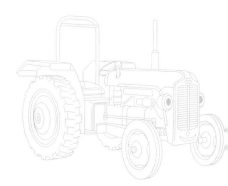

The salesman was surprised. "Our customers usually wait a few days and have their tractors delivered from the factory. Are you sure you want to take it now sir?"

"I am very sure," said Farmer Pete. "I like this tractor very much and I would like to take him now."

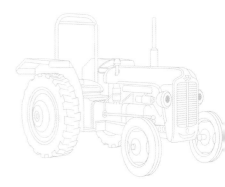

Farmer Pete had to sign lots of forms, whilst the money was being counted.

When everything was completed the salesman handed Farmer Pete the keys to the shiny red tractor. "There you are sir, the tractor is yours. I hope it serves you well for many years."

"I am sure he will," replied Farmer Pete as he climbed into the seat.

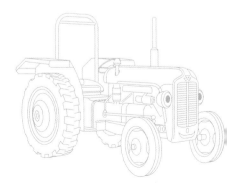

"Now then new tractor, let's see how well you start," said Farmer Pete. He turned the key in the ignition.

"Yes, yes, yes, yes, VROOM", went the tractor as he burst into life.

"Well done," said Farmer Pete. "Now let's see how well you drive."

Farmer Pete carefully drove the Massey Ferguson 35 from the showroom and out onto the road for home.

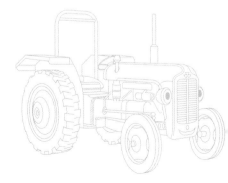

Farmer Pete was very pleased. He drove along the High Street four times and at some roundabouts he went around twice.

When Farmer Pete arrived back at the farm he parked the new tractor in the barn. "Well done," he said. "Welcome to your new home, I know you will be happy here."

Farmer Pete patted the tractor on the bonnet and said, "I shall call you Berty the Thirty, I think that suits you."

Berty the Thirty smiled to himself. He liked his new name and he knew he was going to be happy in his new home.

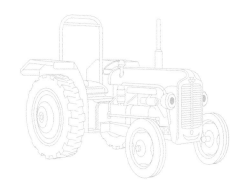

FERGUS' STORY   MR COOMBS THE GAMEKEEPER   GEO
THE MECHANIC   FERGUS GETS A NEW FRIEND   NEVIL
GETS HIS NAME   NEVILLE AND THE HOT AIR BALLOC
FERGUS' BONFIRE NIGHT   FERGUS AT THE BARN FIF
FERGUS AND BERTY CLEAR THE SNOW   FERGUS' CHRISTM/
SPECIAL   THE SPRING TIME SURPRISE   FERGUS AND TH
NEW BUILDING   FERGUS' HALLOWEEN   FERGUS AND TH
STEAM UP   FERGUS AND BERTY GO POTATO PLANTIN
FERGUS AND THE BEAVER SCOUTS   THE WEDDING D/
FERGUS AND THE FLOOD   FERGUS AT THE CIRCUS   FERGU
AND THE HEATWAVE   FERGUS AT THE CARNIVAL   FERGU
AT THE PLOUGHING MATCH   FERGUS AND THE FALLEN TRI
FERGUS' STORY   MR COOMBS THE GAMEKEEPER   GEO
THE MECHANIC   FERGUS GETS A NEW FRIEND   NEVIL
GETS HIS NAME   NEVILLE AND THE HOT AIR BALLOC
FERGUS' BONFIRE NIGHT   FERGUS AT THE BARN FII
FERGUS AND BERTY CLEAR THE SNOW   FERGUS' CHRISTM